To Mabel Grace —J.G.   To Bonnie, who is sweet —N.R.

BACK TO SCHOOL FOR

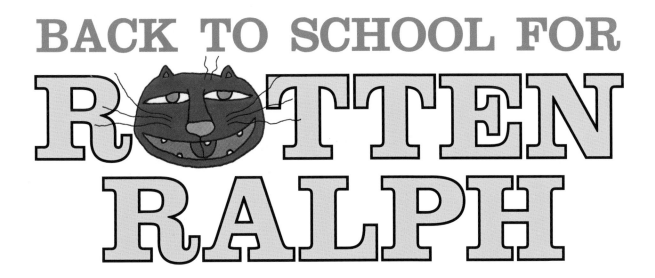

R TTEN RALPH

Written by Jack Gantos • Illustrated by Nicole Rubel

The character of Rotten Ralph was originally created by Jack Gantos and Nicole Rubel.
Back to School for Rotten Ralph. Text copyright © 1998 by Jack Gantos. Illustrations copyright © by Nicole Rubel. Printed in the U.S.A. All rights reserved. Library of Congress Cataloging-in-Publication Data. Gantos, Jack. Back to school for Rotten Ralph / written by Jack Gantos ; illustrated by Nicole Rubel.   p.   cm.   Summary: Afraid of being left alone, Rotten Ralph, the nasty red cat, follows Sarah to school and tries to prevent her from making new friends.   ISBN 0-06-027531-6. — ISBN 0-06-027532-4 (lib. bdg.)   [1. Cats—Fiction.   2. Schools—Fiction.   3. First day of school—Fiction.   4. Friendship—Fiction.]   I. Rubel, Nicole, ill. II. Title. PZ7.G15334Bac 1998 97-49665 [E]—dc21 CIP AC   2   3   4   5   6   7   8   9   10 ❖   Visit us on the World Wide Web! http://www.harperchildrens.com

🏛 HarperCollinsPublishers

Ralph had been rotten all summer long, but Sarah loved him anyway. "I'm so glad I start school tomorrow," said Sarah. She was very excited. "I hope I make some nice new friends."

Rotten Ralph was not excited. He wanted to be Sarah's only friend. He didn't want to be left behind.

He took her book bag. He broke her pencil points. And the next morning when Sarah woke up, Rotten Ralph had turned back the hands on her alarm clocks.

"Ralph!" cried Sarah. "Now I'll be late for school."

When Sarah was in the bathroom, Rotten Ralph pretended to be helpful. He gave her a bar of trick soap.

"Oh, Ralph," said Sarah as she scrubbed her face. "If I'm any later, I'll miss the bus."

"Good," thought Ralph. "Then you can stay home with me."

When Sarah went to put on her new dress,

Rotten Ralph had drawn his face all over the front.

"Ralph," said Sarah, "that's not nice.

Now I'll have to wear my old dress."

When Sarah was dressed, she went searching for her book bag in Rotten Ralph's room. He was lying on his bed. He was foaming at the mouth.

"Ralph," Sarah said with a smile, "you look strange, but you'll be all right."

Finally Sarah was ready to leave the house. But Rotten Ralph was blocking the front door. He was covered with nasty purple spots. His tongue was striped. And he was moaning and groaning.

"Ralph," said Sarah, "stop it. You can't trick me with that fake sickness."

Then she hopped over him and ran out the door.

Rotten Ralph jumped up and followed her. He hid behind a tree as Sarah got on the bus and went to school. Rotten Ralph was left behind. But not for long.

"I can be Sarah's school friend," he said to himself. He went inside and dressed in some of Sarah's clothes. He packed a lunch, then hurried off to school.

When Ralph arrived, it was almost recess time. Sarah knew she would make new friends on the playground. But when she tried to get up, she stumbled. Her shoelaces had been tied together. By the time she untied the knots, recess was over. She didn't make any new friends.

"Everyone choose a book to read with your book buddy," said the librarian during library time.

"Now I'll make a new friend," thought Sarah. But each time she went to choose a book from a shelf, a sneaky hand snatched it from the other side. "Stop that," ordered Sarah.

"Since you can't be quiet," the librarian said to Sarah, "you'll have to sit by yourself."

At lunchtime Sarah sat down next to a friendly-looking girl. "Do you want to share?" asked the girl.

"I'd love to," Sarah replied. But when she opened her lunch bag it was filled with old fish bones.

"Excuse me," said the girl, and ran off holding her nose.

After lunch the class lined up at the water fountain. Rotten Ralph pushed Sarah from behind. She fell forward and knocked everyone down.

"Sarah," said the teacher. "Control yourself."

"Somebody pushed me first," Sarah explained.

"That's no reason to push back," said the

teacher. "Now tell everyone you are sorry."

Toward the end of the day, the teacher went up to Sarah's desk.

"What's going on?" she asked.

"I've had a difficult day," Sarah said. "Every time I try to make a friend, something goes wrong."

"Perhaps you are trying too hard," said the teacher. "Maybe you should wait for a friend to come to you."

Sarah did. During the music lesson she stood alone at the back of the stage. One by one the students took turns singing. When it was Sarah's turn, a strange new boy sneaked up and stood next to her. Each time she opened her mouth to sing, the boy opened his mouth and let out a loud "MEOOOW!"

"Ralph!" Sarah shouted. Now she knew why everything had gone wrong.

Everybody was excited to have a cat in the class. They wanted to get to know Ralph and Sarah.

"Oh no," thought Ralph. He wanted Sarah all to himself. But it was too late. Sarah had made new friends.

At the end of the day Ralph and Sarah went home together. While Sarah did her homework, Rotten Ralph made peanut-butter-and-jelly snacks.

Finally, Sarah made a list of all her new friends. But Rotten Ralph wasn't on the list.

"I have one more friend," she said, turning to Ralph. "Can you guess his name?"

Rotten Ralph jumped onto her lap. He pressed

his messy paw print onto her list.

Sarah smiled. "I made a lot of new friends today.

But you'll always be at the top of my list."

"I'm the best," thought Ralph. Then he purred

and purred.